You Are Growing

→ All the Time ←

Deborah Farmer Kris

Illustrated by Jennifer Zivoin

free spirit

PUBLISHING®

Library of Congress Cataloging-in-Publication Data
Names: Kris, Deborah Farmer, author. | Zivoin, Jennifer, illustrator.
Title: You are growing all the time / Deborah Farmer Kris ; illustrated by Jennifer Zivoin.
Description: Minneapolis, MN : Free Spirit Publishing Inc., 2022. | Series: All the time | Audience: Ages 2–6
Identifiers: LCCN 2021053300 (print) | LCCN 2021053301 (ebook) | ISBN 9781631987090 (hardcover)
    ISBN 9781631987106 (pdf) | ISBN 9781631987113 (epub)
Subjects: CYAC: Stories in rhyme. | Growth—Fiction. | LCGFT: Stories in rhyme. | Picture books.
    Classification: LCC PZ8.3.K888 Yo 2022 (print) | LCC PZ8.3.K888 (ebook) | DDC [E]—dc23
LC record available at https://lccn.loc.gov/2021053300
LC ebook record available at https://lccn.loc.gov/2021053301

Free Spirit Publishing does not have control over or assume responsibility for author or third-party websites and their content.

Parents, teachers, and other adults: We strongly urge you to monitor children's use of the internet.

Edited by Cassie Sitzman
Cover and interior design by Emily Dyer

Printed in China

Free Spirit Publishing
An imprint of Teacher Created Materials
6325 Sandburg Road, Suite 100
Minneapolis, MN 55427-3674
(612) 338-2068
help4kids@freespirit.com
freespirit.com

FSC
www.fsc.org
MIX
Paper from
responsible sources
FSC® C144853

For Fred Rogers and his timeless
example of treating children
with care and dignity

Every year you're taller.
You need new clothes and shoes.

You also grow in other ways,
and that's exciting news!

You are growing
all the time.

Once you crawled on hands and knees—
I'd pluck you off the floor.

Now you run and skip and slide
and pull me out the door.

You are growing all the time.

On tiptoes at the library,
you reach the highest shelf.

And when it's time for checkout,
you hold the books yourself.

You are growing all the time.

You help me set the table,
with forks and cups and plates.

You try a bite of something new,
and tell me it tastes great.

You are growing all the time.

You build magic kingdoms
from blocks and rocks and sand

Your teddies go on noble quests.
Your trucks explore the land.

You are growing all the time.

Your paintings burst with color.
Your knock-knocks make me laugh.

You make up cool new dance moves
like the "slippy-toed giraffe."

You are growing all the time.

I watched you when you lost the game.
You wore an angry frown.

And then I watched you
pause and breathe
and calm that feeling down.

You are growing all the time.

When your friend fell off the swings,
you ran to tell his dad.

And then you drew your friend a card
because he still seemed sad.

You are growing all the time.

You love classroom sharing time.
You listen and you wait.

And when it's time for you to speak,
you smile and stand up straight.

You are growing all the time.

You ask amazing questions.
You flip through stacks of books.

You want to learn to bike and build
and read and write and cook.

You are growing all the time.

Sometimes learning is a breeze.
Sometimes you struggle through it.

You try and think and try again,
and then say, "I can do it!"

You are growing all the time.

You're growing on the outside,
and on the inside too.

You're kind and brave and curious.
I am so proud of you.

You are growing all the time.

ᗃ A Letter to Caregivers ᗃ

The day before kindergarten started, my son was feeling that predictable mix of excitement and nervousness. As I tucked him into bed that night, I told him, "I am so excited for all the books you are going to read this year—and all the words you are going to write, all the pictures you are going to draw, all the structures you are going to build, all the friends you are going to make, and all the ways you will become stronger and more responsible. I love watching you grow!"

That's the thing about kids: they grow. Sometimes they grow so fast that we want to stop time to savor the moment. And while it's easy to see how they are growing physically, what they need us to notice most are all the ways they are "growing on the inside."

That's a phrase I borrowed from Fred Rogers, to whom this book is dedicated. He wrote, "'Growing on the inside' are the words I use when I talk with children about such things as learning to wait,

learning to keep on trying, being able to talk about their feelings, and to express those feelings in constructive ways. These signs of growth need at least as much notice and applause as the outward kind, and children need to feel proud of them."

In the spirit of Mr. Rogers, here are a few ways to do just that.

Five Ways to Notice and Applaud Children's Growth

1. Celebrate Signs of Growth

In the early childhood years, every month seems filled with changes. What are the little things children can do now that they couldn't do a few months ago? Zip up their jacket? Put away their clothes? Help walk the dog? Name their colors? Write their name? Use their words to tell what they need? Share toys and play cooperatively?

When you see these signs of growth, say so: "You just put on your snow pants all by yourself. You couldn't do that last year!" Make it a bedtime or mealtime ritual to point out one good thing you noticed that day about your child.

2. Acknowledge Their Effort

Sometimes new learning comes easily . . . and sometimes it doesn't. Learning new skills takes time and effort—and that can be frustrating for children. As my son once said, "I don't want to *learn* how to ride a bike, I want to *know* how to ride a bike!" Every child struggles with something—whether it's learning their letters, tying their shoes, or finding ways to settle big emotions. When frustrations arise, your steady support can encourage children to persevere:

- Be patient and acknowledge their effort: "Putting on shoes by yourself can be tough! I'm so proud of you for trying over and over again."

- Break it down. Give children an entry point to a challenging task. Instead of saying, "Time to clean your room," try saying, "Let's start by picking up all the books and putting them back in the basket."

- Express your confidence in them: "I know this is hard, but I know you can do it. I'm here to help if you need me."

- Harness the power of *yet*, and model its use. There's a big difference, emotionally, between the phrases "I can't do it!" and "I can't do it, yet." The word *yet* is a bridge between present frustration and future possibility.

3. Give Them Age-Appropriate Responsibilities

Early childhood is a great time to introduce chores and responsibilities—because young children are eager to be helpers! Not only do chores help children learn practical skills, but they also support school readiness.

For example, sorting and classifying are math skills that children practice as they sort laundry or put away silverware or toys. Also, think about the mental attention and motor skills it takes to use a spray bottle, set a table, peel oranges for lunch, spread butter on bread, or sweep a room.

And engaging in chores doesn't just build useful skills—it also builds kindness and helps children feel that their work matters. "There is a strong link between doing things that are good for the whole family and the development of generous behavior," science journalist Melinda Wenner Moyer told me. "When I ask my kids to help clear the table, I might say, 'This is

really helping me and Dad out because we have a lot going on. You're making our house look nicer, and you're making it so that we have clean dishes for breakfast tomorrow. It's so helpful for the entire family." Children can find genuine satisfaction in contributing to family or classroom life and in being seen as responsible.

4. Preview What's to Come

I have a friend who, around her children's birthdays each year, takes time to preview with them some of the new skills they will be learning that year. As she told me, "We sit down and review the skills that they should have learned that year and what they will be learning in the coming year. We try to make it celebratory: 'Wow, you learned to make your own lunch, wipe off the table, sweep, and clean windows this year! This coming year, you'll learn to sew a button, make grilled cheese, and clean a bathroom. You are growing up!'"

5. Name Character Traits

We all want our kids to grow up to be kind, responsible, and brave. We can support their character development by pointing out actions that build these good habits. Linking their efforts to specific words can be empowering. For example:

- "You checked on your friend when she fell down. That was really kind."

- "You fed the dog without being asked. That was so responsible of you!"

- "Thank you for telling me you broke the mug. That was honest and brave."

When we recognize and celebrate all the ways our kids are learning and growing, we help them develop the confidence they need to continue to grow up strong.

—Deborah Farmer Kris

⇒About the Author and Illustrator⇐

Deborah Farmer Kris is a child development expert and parent educator. She serves as a columnist and consultant for PBS KIDS and writes for NPR's *MindShift* and other national publications. Over the course of her career, Deborah has taught almost every grade K–12, served as a school administrator, directed leadership institutes, and presented to hundreds of parents and educators around the United States. Deborah and her husband live in Massachusetts with their two kids—who love to test every theory she's ever had about child development. Mostly, she loves sharing nuggets of practical wisdom that can help kids and families thrive.

Jennifer Zivoin has illustrated more than forty children's books, and her art has appeared in children's magazines, including *High Five* and *Clubhouse Jr.* She illustrated the *New York Times* and #1 *Indiebound* best seller *Something Happened in Our Town.* The Children's Museum of Indianapolis, the world's largest children's museum, featured her art in a special *Pirates and Princesses* exhibit. Jennifer provided artwork for celebrity picture books, including those by James Patterson and Guns N' Roses. Recently, Jennifer made her debut as an author with her book *Pooka & Bunni.* Jennifer lives in Indiana with her husband, daughters, and pet chinchillas.

Great Books from Free Spirit's All the Time Series

Written from the perspective of an adult speaking to a child, these whimsical rhyming books help young children know that they are deserving of love through life's ups and downs. This encouraging series shows them all the ways they're supported as they continue to grow and learn. *32 pp.; color illust.; 10" x 10"; ages 2–6*

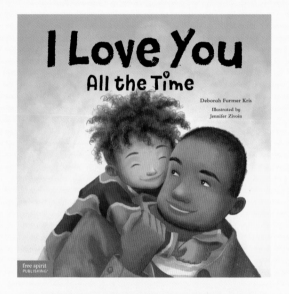

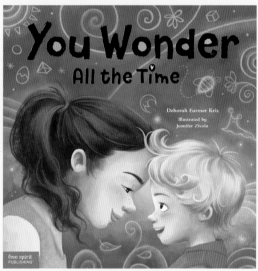